The Rabbit Story

To my wife, Blossom Budney

First Edition   1 2 3 4 5 6 7 8 9 10

Library of Congress Cataloging in Publication Data
Tresselt, Alvin R. The rabbit story.
Summary: A young rabbit is born, grows up with her brothers and sisters, is caught by a farmer
and kept in a pen by her little boy, and finally escapes to return to the free life of other wild rabbits.
1. Rabbits—Juvenile fiction.   [1. Rabbits—Fiction]   I. Ewing, C.S., ill.   II. Title.   PZ10.3.T77Rab
1989   [E]   88-32594
ISBN 0-688-08650-0   ISBN 0-688-08651-9 (lib. bdg.)

The Rabbit Story

ALVIN TRESSELT

PICTURES BY CAROLYN EWING

Lothrop, Lee & Shepard Books   New York

Deep in a fur-lined burrow,
lined with soft warm fur from their mother,
the little rabbits were born.
So carefully had the mother hidden her nest on the edge
of the meadow that no one could find it.

Safe inside their snug nest, she fed her babies,
as the silent owl flew past on velvety wings,
looking for his supper.

So fast the babies grew!
At first they had no fur, and their eyes,
like the eyes of kittens, were tight shut.

When Mother Rabbit went off to nibble sweet clover,
the little ones huddled together in the fur-lined warmth and slept.
But soon their eyes opened.
Soon they grew their own warm coats of rabbit fur.
And soon, as their legs grew stronger, they were hopping about
in their home.

Now the babies learned what a rabbit must know.
Beware the swift-running fox…
The hungry weasel…
The velvet-winged owl…

Be careful...watch out!
Run fast...stand still!
Hide and listen with your long long ears.
And watch for the farmer and his dog.

But the little rabbits were carefree in their fresh green world.
They tumbled in the grass, then sat still as statues.
They thumped their strong rabbit legs
and hopped over tree trunks.

Then they scampered under bushes—quick-as-a-wink!
And that's how the baby rabbits
learned to take care of themselves.

At last the snug little burrow grew too small.
One by one the babies hopped away to live a rabbit life.
Little Rabbit hopped this way and that.
Past the field mice in their secret runways in the meadow grass.
Past the noisy squirrels frisking up and down the trees.
She followed her sniffing, wiggly nose and nibbled
on the spring grass and clover.

Then early one morning Little Rabbit discovered the best food of all.
Long rows of tender lettuce and young beans.
Tasty cabbage plants and new carrots.
But once, as she slipped under the fence of the garden,
her foot caught in a piece of string.
Bang! Down over the little rabbit came a box.
Little Rabbit knew about foxes and weasels, owls and dogs,
but she didn't know about traps.

Little Rabbit sat very still as the day grew brighter. Suddenly, she felt the tiny earth-shake that told her someone was coming near.

It was the farmer, and he grinned as he lifted the rabbit out of the trap. "So you're the one who's been growing fat on my vegetables," he said. "But you're only a baby!"

He carried the little rabbit to his barn and put her in a cage.
Soon he came back with a boy.
"There she is," said the farmer to his son.
"If you want her for a pet, see that you take good care of her.
Just don't let her loose to finish off my garden."
The boy brought fresh grass and water for his pet.
But Little Rabbit just crouched in a corner and wiggled her nose.

As the days passed, Little Rabbit grew used to the boy,
and soon he could let her out of her cage.
Then, as she followed behind him, the curious hens
clucked and gossiped together about this strange wild animal
in their barnyard.

Slowly the long summer slipped into crisp September weather.
Now in the frosty mornings the crows cawed from the swampland,
and the south-bound geese honked overhead.
Little Rabbit sniffed the misty autumn air
and she felt a yearning for the wild free life she had known.

One evening, after the boy had fed his rabbit,
she discovered the door of the cage was not shut tight.
With a push and a wiggle Little Rabbit found herself outside.
She followed her nose across the sleeping barnyard,
past the frostbitten vegetable garden,
over the stubbly meadow,
into the thickets beside the woods.
And there Little Rabbit joined the free life of the wild rabbits.

Through the long cold winter she hopped about in the snow
as best she could, finding bits to eat.
The soft tender bark of young trees,
weed seeds, withered berries, and frozen corn in the farmer's fields.

But at last the soft warm winds returned from the south.
The days grew longer, and once more the meadow turned green
with new grass and clover to eat.
Once more the father rabbits thumped the ground
with their long strong legs, calling their mates.

Then one day Little Rabbit dug a burrow beside the meadow,
carefully hidden so no one could find it.
She cushioned it with grass, and lined it
with soft warm fur from her body.
And as the wood thrush sang his evening song,
the mother rabbit fed her new babies in their snug nest
at the edge of the meadow.

Alvin Tresselt writes for very young children in a very special way. Using the simplest, clearest language, he introduces the reader to the basic facts and moods of the natural world. Noted for the poetic quality of the author's prose, his books have awakened thousands of readers and listeners to the many small miracles of life. *Rain Drop Splash,* with illustrations by Leonard Weisgard, was a Caldecott Honor Book in 1946, and *White Snow, Bright Snow,* illustrated by Roger Duvoisin, was the winner of the 1947 Caldecott Medal. *The Rabbit Story* was first published in 1957 with illustrations by Leonard Weisgard. Mr. Tresselt has updated the text of this new edition, enhancing its appeal to a modern generation of children. Carolyn Ewing's illustrations, accomplished in watercolor on illustration board, add to the timely and timeless quality of this new edition. Mr. Tresselt lives in Redding, Connecticut. Ms. Ewing lives in Kansas City, Missouri.